# Bloom: Growth in the Unexpected Place

ISBN: 979-8-9989568-2-9

# Bloom: Growth in the Unexpected Place

# Foreword by Deborah Holt Noel

I had just emceed a youth oratorical contest in Thomasville and received unexpected recognition and an award. As a television producer and series host for PBS North Carolina, I'm often called to shine a light on others. That night was no different—I was sharing the excitement of teen contestants exchanging hugs and posing with their trophies—when a woman approached me. She introduced herself, complimented my performance that evening, and handed me her card. She explained how she could help me expand what I had just done into something more lucrative.

It was an invitation that aligned perfectly with something I had recently been tossing around in my mind but didn't quite know how to leap toward. She planted that seed at just the right time and place. Soon, I found myself seated at her kitchen table, listening intently—more than an hour from my own home, in a stranger's home.

Looking back, I can't believe I just rolled up to this woman's house without concern for my safety. I didn't know her—as they say—from Adam's house cat. I consider myself a cautious and smart person, and yet, there I was. But my willingness to be there probably says more about her than it does about me.

Dr. Timogi Jackson spoke to me like a dear friend who could see into the future—and was eager to share an insight that might be a doorway to something good. I waited for her to tell me how much this would cost, but that moment never came. I listened for the "deal"—the part where I was supposed to make some investment to unlock a promise. But the only investment she named was my faith, time, and talent.

Before I left her home, she gave me several of her books, invited me to an upcoming event, and made a few recommendations for next steps. A year later, after plenty of time to reflect on that encounter, I ran into her again. She didn't shame or embarrass me for not being in touch. Instead, we shared that familiar, "Girl, it's been so long—let's reconnect soon" kind of moment, the one that recognizes we're all busy, so we're all good. We eventually did reconnect by phone, and her tone hadn't changed—though this time she offered even more specific guidance.

My interactions with Dr. Jackson have been few, but I get the distinct feeling she is the real deal. She not only speaks with authority but with the conviction of a woman who's lived it. Anyone who has raised children understands the aching desire to spare them from heartbreak—especially when they're just not ready to believe you. In her eyes, Dr. Timogi carries the look of a mother who wishes you would believe her when she says, "I can help you do your next great thing."

That day at her table, Dr. Jackson shared pieces of her personal story: a journey marked by unfairness, heartbreak, disappointments, and setbacks. She spoke freely of her valleys and what she learned there. The muscles she built digging out of those valleys are now the very tools she shares with others who feel stuck—unable even to look toward the peaks.

In telling her story, speaking it aloud, she has found herself surrounded by a circle of like-minded women drawn to her through shared experience— women who've scaled their own mountains with tools of their own. We've all heard "misery loves company," but joy and perspective do, too.

# Bloom: Growth in the Unexpected Place

Whether we're ready to admit it or not, we all thrive on connection. We all feel a little more hopeful when we meet others walking through what we, too, have endured.

*Bloom* is that tribe—a collection of voices from women you'll likely click with. Maybe it's someone who grew up in a household just like yours, or someone who wrestled with the same fear, or someone who carries a resilience you admire and want to tap into.

Within these pages, I invite you to find connection. Because so often, simply knowing you're not alone becomes the firm ground we need to stand up and move forward. The book shares Dr. Timogi's own reflection—a story that's compelling because it's so common and familiar.

Dr. Jackson believes in spiritual and financial freedom and independence for every woman. Her life's work is to create tools and pathways to help the sisters she meets claim that freedom for themselves. Why? Because it feels so good.

# Bloom: Growth in the Unexpected Place

It is my hope that you will see yourself in these stories—told by everyday women just like you—and that their experiences will uplift, strengthen, and inspire you toward your next achievement.

*Deborah Holt Noel*

1. **Bloom when a seed of possibility is planted at just the right time.**
   Sometimes alignment shows up as a conversation, an invitation, or a nudge that affirms what your spirit has already been sensing.
2. **Bloom when faith becomes your only required investment.**
   True guidance doesn't always come with a price tag—it often comes from someone who sees your potential and simply wants to help you rise.
3. **Bloom through shared stories that remind you you're not alone.**
   Healing, growth, and courage are contagious in the presence of women who've turned their valleys into victories—and are willing to walk with you through yours.

# Bloom: Growth in the Unexpected Place

**Series Host & Executive Producer,
PBS North Carolina**

***Deborah Holt Noel*** *is a multifaceted content creator, producer, and on-air personality at PBS North Carolina. As the host of the popular and Emmy-nominated weekly travel series, North Carolina Weekend, she journeys across the state, unveiling its rich tapestry of historical sites, scenic landscapes, iconic attractions, cultural treasures, and culinary delights. In her role as executive producer of the enduring public affairs program, Black Issues Forum, Deborah leverages her extensive previous experience as host and producer to steer the production team towards thought-provoking discussions. Outside of work, Deborah enjoys leisure time as a wife and mother.*

***www.deborahholtnoel.com***

*Left to Right Deborah Holt Noel and Dr. Timogi at the one **"year later, after plenty of time to reflect on that encounter"** event in 2024 referenced in the Foreword.*

# Contents

# Introduction: Flowers are Not Delicate

There is something supernatural about waking up, going outside, and seeing that a new flower has bloomed. Yesterday there was nothing there—but today, suddenly, from nowhere, a flower appeared. You do not have to be a gardener to know that a flower doesn't just appear from nowhere.

In reality, we know that some time ago, a seed was planted in the ground. And, that seed had to lay in the darkness beneath the sound and weight of trampling feet, dogs relieving themselves, warm days, cold nights, the rain, and wind.

Flowers are not delicate.

That seed had to break free, push itself open, and spread—essentially destroying its shell, which meant destroying its protection and safety in a dark, loud, and heavy world. Then, that seed, in its brokenness had to push further down into the deep, dark, dirt.

# Bloom: Growth in the Unexpected Place

Flowers are not delicate.

Is the seed lost? Is the seed confused? Did the seed listen to a podcaster with no knowledge or credentials—experiential or theoretical, and follow their advice into oblivion? No.

That seed, over time—had to ground itself, secure its roots, and firmly grasp the soil beneath it—then, it had to muster all its strength and push up.

Up through the weight.
Up through the dirt.
Up through the darkness.
Up through the noise.
Up through the unknown.
Until one day, it broke through the soil to behold the light above.

Flowers are not delicate.

Once that seed received just a little glimpse of sun—shining and beaming upon the small stem that had emerged from down below—it realized there were no limits to what it could do. That stem began

# Bloom: Growth in the Unexpected Place

to further reach for the sun. As a result, it eventually became a bud.

Wrapped in the leaves of the bud, that seed lay in the darkness, again. Decisions, decisions. Will the seed stop there? It had already conquered darkness and the unknown before. Will it refuse to let the forces of darkness stop it from blooming? No, the answer is no. This time not only will it push and spread, this time, when it pushes out of the bud— and it blooms you will call her by her name, Flower.

Flowers are not delicate.

You will marvel at her splendor. You will become enchanted by her fragrance. You will want to see her as often as possible. You will want her at every function and holiday to show her off to your family and friends.

Bloom.

Bloom not because you know what's on the other side, but because you *deserve* to know what's on

# Bloom: Growth in the Unexpected Place

the other side.

Bloom when life gets heavy.
Bloom when life is dark.
Bloom when life gets loud.
Bloom when it feels like you're going backwards—
but you're really building roots and securing a
foundation for your purpose.

Bloom, despite what it feels like to push.
Bloom because you *can* push. And, that push—the
one that feels impossible—that's the one that will
change your circumstances, build your resilience,
and cause you to reach relentlessly for the sun.

Bloom not because you know what's on the other
side, but because you *can create* what's on the
other side.

Flowers are not delicate. Bloom.

Dr. *Timogi*

# 1. Tishember: The Month That Changed Everything

Junior year in undergrad was supposed to be a turning point; it was my first time rooming with the friends I'd met freshman year. We survived dorm life and late-night study sessions, and now we were moving into a space together, ready to make more memories. I imagined laughter-filled nights, shared meals, and sisterhood.

The semester started in August, but everything shifted in September, a month I always celebrated as "Tishember," a playful nod to my birthday and the joy I brought to my circle of friends throughout the month. That year on the weekend of my birthday, joy turned into grief in the most unimaginable way. One Sunday, twenty-four hours before I turned 20, my father was murdered.

I couldn't process the weight of it. I didn't know

how. So, the next morning, I did the only thing I knew to do. I got up and went to class. My heart was broken but I thought if I stayed in motion, maybe I wouldn't fall apart.

Grief didn't ask me if I was ready. It just arrived and sat with me. And while I tried to carry it quietly, it began affecting every corner of my life, including my relationships with my roommates. I stopped talking because I didn't know how to express what I was going through. I didn't want to explain my tears or to be asked why I wasn't smiling. I just needed space.

But instead of understanding, they gave me distance. Instead of asking if I was okay, they whispered about me. I overheard pieces of conversation and sensed the shift into judgment where there should have been grace. Some even suggested I had motives for pulling away. But what I needed wasn't speculation. I needed support.

My mother, sensing that I was trying to hold too much on my own, stepped in. She emailed my professors, advisor, and school counselor, letting them know what had happened, just in case I needed time or space. She reminded me I didn't have to prove anything and that I could pause if I needed to. She also reminded me she believed in me and that made all the difference. I decided to keep going. Quietly. Painfully. Purposefully.

That season taught me what resilience really looks like. It's not loud or glamorous. It's showing up when everything in you wants to lie down. It's turning in assignments with tears on your keyboard. It's walking through sorrow and still holding on to your goals.

Despite the heartbreak, I graduated a semester early with a B.S. in Information Science, earning honors. Crossing that stage was more than a personal achievement; it was a sacred moment of triumph over tragedy. Every late night, every tear, every step I took while carrying grief on my back, it all led to that moment.

But something inside me had shifted. Losing my

# Bloom: Growth in the Unexpected Place

father released something deep within me that craved meaning, peace, and a world wider than the one I knew. I wanted to step outside the pain and experience life beyond its boundaries.

Six months after my tragic loss, I took my first international trip to Dubai with my best friend. That trip changed everything. For the first time in a long time, I felt free. I felt alive. And I felt my father's strength with me, reminding me that life was worth exploring.

Since then, I've traveled to over 10 countries across four continents, from the Caribbean to Africa, Europe, and the Middle East. I've danced in the streets of Egypt, worked with youth in Barbados, sipped tea in the Dominican Republic, and coordinated culture-centered trips with my family and friends. My loss made me want to live louder. Travel became my therapy, my education, and my celebration of resilience.

I am committed to creating opportunities for others, especially young people, to see the world, expand their horizons, and grow through global experiences. My career path shifted from merely checking boxes to making a meaningful impact. I wasn't just surviving anymore; I was becoming.

I don't look back on that season with bitterness anymore. I see it as a chapter that tested everything I thought I knew about strength, but that episode showed me I had more in me than I realized.

**Tishember** will never be the same. It's no longer just a celebration of my birth but a reminder of what I've survived. A sacred mix of grief and gratitude. A moment where life attempted to break me, and I still chose to bloom.

*Tishana Jackson*

1. *Bloom, sometimes resilience is built in silence and sorrow.*

2. *Bloom, loss can awaken a longing to live louder.*

3. *Bloom, support gives you space to heal, not pressure to perform.*

# Bloom: Growth in the Unexpected Place

**Tishana Jackson** *holds a B.S. in Information Science from UNCG and a master's in interactive media from Elon University. She serves as Coordinator of International Programs and Study Abroad at Winston-Salem State University, where she fosters global engagement and student growth. Tishana is also a creative entrepreneur, owning a business inspired by Trinity Grace Photography and TriniTeas, a specialty coffee, tea, and boba brand. Passionate about culture, connection, and creativity, she blends her academic, artistic, and entrepreneurial pursuits to inspire others and make a meaningful impact locally and globally.*

*www.tishanajackson.com*

# 2. Stop Waiting for Permission

Have you ever felt paralyzed, awaiting permission to proceed? Enduring the frustrating silence of exclusion, your voice unheard, your perspective ignored, passively observing instead of actively shaping your destiny?

Early in my professional journey, I felt the sting of inequitable treatment. I observed my District Manager's meticulous attention to a colleague's territory, a stark contrast to the cursory review of my own. The disparity gnawed at me; I questioned the discrepancy, searching for the explanation for this treatment.

One day, that same colleague came into my area, and the District Manager once again took time to give my coworker all the time she needed. My Specialist knew something was wrong; that there

# Bloom: Growth in the Unexpected Place

was something on my mind. My Specialist asked and I explained that I didn't understand why the District Manager was spending so much time with my peer and not with me. The rest of the team was on the other side in a huddle, and I wasn't included.

My Specialist said, "If you want to know what's being said, go ahead and walk over there and join the huddle to find out." I looked at my specialist and said, "Are you serious?" "Just walk right up." My Specialist said "yes, go ahead. I'll give you a few minutes, and then I'll come get you." I said, "okay, I'm going over there."

I walked over and squeezed into the circle to listen to what was being discussed. No one really noticed me, I thought at the time. After a while, I felt a tap on my shoulder and as I looked over, my Specialist said, "okay, let's go."

As we walked, my Specialist said, "Are you good? Did that make you feel better?" I said "yes, it did." "Thank you for allowing me to do that."

# Bloom: Growth in the Unexpected Place

My expert declared, approvingly, that future inquiries regarding ongoing projects or inclusions require no prior authorization. Your exceptional abilities are undeniable. If you require more direct oversight from the District Manager, don't hesitate to seek it out assertively; proactive engagement is not merely advisable; it's essential. Take a commanding role; claim your rightful position at the table. "Now, let's finish our walk".

A sudden clarity struck me: permission was not needed. Passive expectations only obstructed advancement and curtailed my influence. True leadership demands you be proactive and determined, self-belief, and complete accountability for one's choices and deeds. This fundamental shift—embracing a growth mindset—is crucial for assertive leadership, fostering empowerment within ourselves and inspiring it in others.

Why is waiting for permission holding leaders back from reaching their full potential? First, it discourages innovation.

# Bloom: Growth in the Unexpected Place

Second, relying on validation can lead to a lack of ownership and create a dependency on one person making decisions. Third, waiting for permission can result in lost opportunities. Fourth, seeking approval can cause a leader to lose confidence.

Liberate yourself from the shackles of permission. Begin by cultivating unwavering self-belief and trusting your intuition; embrace your authentic self completely. Shed the restrictive limitations of a fixed mindset and cultivate a growth-oriented perspective. This transformative shift enables leaders to confront challenges with confidence, embracing continuous learning, unwavering commitment, and tenacious resilience.

Seize the reins of initiative; proactively shape your destiny rather than passively awaiting direction. Learn from missteps, viewing setbacks not as defeats but as invaluable opportunities for profound personal and professional advancement. Finally, empower your team, fostering a culture of decisive action and shared responsibility. This

# Bloom: Growth in the Unexpected Place

proactive approach to leadership projects a commanding presence, radiating confidence, initiative, and an empowering influence.

This transformative experience instilled in me a profound self-assurance and unshakeable trust in my leadership capabilities. I no longer sought validation or yearned for a sense of belonging; instead, my presence commanded respect. My position felt inherently mine, a responsibility I embraced without hesitation. The imperative was simple: proceed.

This wasn't merely a tactic; it was a fundamental shift in perspective. I projected self-possession and accountability, commanding my space with resolute conviction and unwavering self-belief.

A crippling dependence on external validation frequently stifles the pursuit of ambition. This hesitancy to take the reins and assume leadership over one's own destiny profoundly restricts personal growth and prevents the realization of a

# Bloom: Growth in the Unexpected Place

truly fulfilling existence.

Bloom by doing three things to stop waiting for permission to lead:

1. Focus on taking the initiative—leaders who bloom are driven by their commitment.
2. Seek opportunities and trust your abilities.
3. Empower yourself to build confidence and embrace setbacks as growth, not a reason to stop growing.

Take your seat at the table.

*Madelina Fordham*

1. *Bloom when you stop waiting and start walking toward inclusion.*
2. *Bloom when self-belief overpowers the need for permission.*
3. *Bloom when you lead without waiting to be invited.*

# Bloom: Growth in the Unexpected Place

**Madelina Fordham**
**Regional Director of Operations**

*Madelina Fordham, a seasoned retail executive boasting a three-decade career, has relocated from Vineland, New Jersey, to Winston-Salem, North Carolina. In her current role as Regional Operations Director, she leverages her extensive experiences and profound insights as a Certified Professional Life Coach. Furthermore, she is a celebrated co-author of "Illuminate—Stories of Empowerment Lighting the Path for Women in Life, Love and Business. Her remarkable achievements include two prestigious Top Woman in Grocery Awards, bestowed upon her in 2016 and 2024, a testament to her exceptional leadership and unwavering commitment to excellence.*

**www.linkedin.com/in/madelina-fordham**
**www.instagram.com/madelinafordham**

# 3. Built Between Two Rhythms

I didn't grow up with a single rhythm.

My childhood unfolded between homes, between parents, and between expectations of what life *should* be and what it *was*. When I was at the age of six my parents separated. I learned early that love and stability don't always arrive in one package. I became fluent in dual realities, two sets of routines, two communication styles, two emotional landscapes: two rhythms.

My mother's rhythm, like most, was more nurturing in her communication style, and emotionally, she was always committed to including us primarily in her decisions and actions. My father's rhythm was different. Like many Nigerian fathers, he was strict and reserved, still guided by an old-fashioned, traditional Nigerian mindset when making decisions.

# Bloom: Growth in the Unexpected Place

The back-and-forth wasn't easy. It meant packing bags weekly, navigating shifting rules, and learning when to speak and when to listen. As I grew, I assimilated in both environments at a pace that curated my endurance today; I learned their rhythms. I quickly became aware that the way I held simple conversations with my mother had to be reformatted when I had those same conversations with my father. What felt like fragmentation at first, eventually formed the blueprint for my strength and my own rhythm.

Through navigating to Mom's rhythm one week and Dad's the next, I developed skills that no classroom could teach: emotional regulation, flexibility, and empathy. I learned how to communicate my responsibilities to professors, maintain my professional responsibilities, and take advantage of the very resources I was recommending to those around me. I became someone who could adapt quickly and meet people where they were because I had lived that day in and day out since I was six years old.

# Bloom: Growth in the Unexpected Place

I remember when I went to my high school prom, and I reached out to my father to see if he could help me cover some of the expenses associated with the event. Though grateful for his efforts, I remember not necessarily being able to use his "gratitude" to even cover my hair.

I remember my mother, there with me physically, seeing how all the small things added up in costs. I remember her helping me to the best of her ability. I remember being conflicted about how to explain to my dad things that he wouldn't understand. I remember coming to the realization that if he had been there to see me off, it would have given him a better understanding of what "prom costs" consist of in totality: hair, a dress, a rental car, nails, accessories, makeup, shoes, dinner and the prom ticket itself! Perhaps this had nothing to do with prom and more about being present.

Years later, in my twenties, in the spring of 2023, those skills were put to the test again. While my transcript shows it was my worst academic

# Bloom: Growth in the Unexpected Place

semester, it fails to capture the quiet strength it took to get through it. There was a deep and noticeable shift in my mom's mood and behavior. I worked extra shifts to help offset some of the financial challenges my mother was experiencing.

There were times I missed lectures to be present to support my mother by being emotionally available. I didn't always get the grade, but I showed up not just for her but for myself and the promise of a better future. Looking back, I no longer wish for a different childhood. What once felt like instability revealed itself as a source of resilience. The two distinct rhythms suddenly merged into one melody for me.

My lived experience gave me a lens of compassion that now guides my desire to serve others, particularly children and families, navigating difficult circumstances. I know what it means to face challenges early and still grow. I carry that truth with me, not as baggage, but as armor. Transformation isn't always dramatic. Sometimes,

## Bloom: Growth in the Unexpected Place

it's built slowly, between homes, between moments of hardship, and in the quiet decision to keep going no matter the rhythm of the drum.

*Azy Iheagwara*

1. *Bloom when life gives you two rhythms to master.*
2. *Bloom when presence matters more than provision.*
3. *Bloom when quiet strength carries you through chaos.*

# Bloom: Growth in the Unexpected Place

*Azy Iheagwara*, *a proud Nigerian-American born and raised in Minnesota's Twin Cities, earned a Bachelor of Science in Human Development and Family Studies with a concentration in Child Development, along with minors in Chemistry and Biology. She is deeply committed to advancing equity in pediatric healthcare and aspires to bridge disparities affecting underserved communities. Through a holistic and child-centered approach, she aims to promote accessible, high-quality care for all children, regardless of background.*

# 4. Stuck to Surrendered: How the S.O.A.R. Framework Changed My Life

Loss is something I pray you never have to face, yet it's something I know too well. Grief met me early. At just twelve years old, I lost my mother- my everything. She was my protector, my nurturer, my world. My father lived in the States, so she was the one who carried me through life. When we finally moved to the U.S., I believed life was just beginning. I thought we'd have time. But within a year of our move, she was gone.

I came home from school that day to a dark, heavy atmosphere. Then the words: "Mommy is gone." I watched my father sob like a child, and I stood there—shocked, numb, broken. I couldn't understand. I prayed. I believed we would be together forever! But, —God took her. And I couldn't understand why.

I searched for answers. I needed to see my mother's medical records to help me find them. I visited every hospital she had gone to, only to be told the records had been archived—gone, just like her. And I was once again left in silence.

Then came the COVID-19 pandemic—a season of unimaginable pain. In just one year, I lost five more family members. Each loss reopened wounds I thought had healed. My heart bled, my tears dried, and I slipped into a quiet storm of numbness, anger, and disbelief. It felt like a plague was sweeping through my lineage, and I couldn't stop it.

For a long time, I was trapped spiritually, mentally, and emotionally. I wore strength like a facade, but inside, I was crumbling. I didn't want to live in bitterness, but I didn't know how to heal. Then I stumbled back into the presence of God, not through perfect prayers, but through desperation. I started listening to sermons on how to surrender and heal, and something shifted. It didn't happen overnight, but slowly, I began to feel again. Hope began to glimmer.

I realized that healing didn't start with getting answers; it started with surrender. That's where my personal transformation began. That's where my S.O.A.R. Framework was born—a path that helped me move from grief-stricken and stuck to healing and rising.

## S.O.A.R. Framework

### S – Surrender the Weight

You don't have to carry everything. Surrender isn't giving up—it's letting go of what was never yours to hold: grief, guilt, shame, timelines, or trauma. God never asked you to be strong on your own. Let Him carry you.

### O – Own Your Story

Your story matters—every broken, unfiltered part. Stop hiding it. Stop apologizing for it. God doesn't anoint the edited version; He uses the real you! Your story is the platform he will use to bless others.

## A – Align with God's Vision

Purpose doesn't come from pressure or performance. It comes from alignment. Get quiet. Get still. Ask God: "What do You see in me?" You don't need to chase clarity—just follow His voice, one obedient step at a time.

## R – Rise with Boldness

Boldness isn't noise—it's obedience. Rise even if you're unsure. Say yes to the unknown. You may not have all the answers, but faith isn't about certainty—it's about surrendering to God's plan and trusting it will be greater than your pain.

To the woman reading this who's silently grieving... To the sister feeling stuck between faith and fear... To the mother who's exhausted from being strong for everyone else...

## Bloom: Growth in the Unexpected Place

I see you.

God sees you.

And you are not forgotten.

Your pain is real, but so is your purpose.

Your brokenness is valid, but so is your breakthrough.

Don't let what happened to you define what God is about to do through you.

It's time to release the weight.

It's time to surrender your timeline and trust Him.

It's time to S.O.A.R.

*Joyce Awuro-Tani*

1. *Bloom when grief demands surrender, not strength.*
2. *Bloom when your unedited story becomes someone else's healing.*
3. *Bloom when faith leads you where natural answers cannot.*

# Bloom: Growth in the Unexpected Place

*Joyce Awuro-Tani is an acclaimed MC, Speaker, Moderator, Host, Facilitator and the founder of Grace and Growth Gathering, a faith-filled community for women believing that every woman carries a story of resilience, triumph, and unwavering faith. Women navigating life's transitions or seeking clarity in their God-given purpose, have a place to grow, connect, and thrive. She has hosted events for the City of Laurel, Anne Arundel County, and recently International motivational Speaker Dr. Cheryl Wood's 2024 SPEAKERCon Conference. She speaks on topics on The Power of Purpose and Alignment, "Is this it"? When Purpose Feels Foggy and her S.O.A.R Framework.*

**www.mceejt.com**
**www.graceandgrowthgathering.com**

# 5. Prepared Purpose: How Did I Get Here?

What am I doing here?

I was not confused, I was stunned. I, R. Folice Bailey, have coached leaders, inspired others, led worship and schools, and stood strong in storms. Folice -- educated, intelligent, discerning, successful, spirit-filled and *saved*—was in an abusive relationship, a psychological prison, an emotional entanglement.

Relationships. The proverbial thorn in my flesh.

I warred about ending the relationship with a man for whom I cared for deeply. The hurt was numbing; I declared what I now realize cracked open a dangerous door: "I'm done." Those words, that inner vow, were uttered from a place of brokenness. Numbness. That broken numbness became the perfect hiding place for the inimical deception. Preparing for our upcoming worship event, the beguiling minstrel counseled, "Is that the type of relationship you want and believe you deserve?" "No," I answered. Weeks later, I walked away.

What I walked into next did not look like abuse. It looked like encouragement. Support. A male perspective. Afterall, I *was still single*, never married, and had ended another two-year relationship. It felt like brotherly love, genuine concern, authentic care.

I was not looking for another relationship. I was done. Done hoping. Done waiting to be *found*. Done believing the marriage prophesies. Done opening my heart to those who did not know how to value it. I was numb, done, and cared less.

Walking numbly, I faltered. I walked right into a relationship where my strengths were studied, and my compassion weaponized. The emotional abuse was surgical -- slow, strategic, and calculated. The psychological control -- masterful. It slowly eroded my boundaries and my peace. It compromised my

# Bloom: Growth in the Unexpected Place

worth and silenced my voice.

This oppressor, charming and calculating, wrapped control in comments and cloaked manipulation in need. He did not yell, he jokingly condemned. He did not hit, he hand-crafted harmed. He exploited my empathy, twisted my loyalty, and drained my finances.

My empathic heart, nurturing desire, intellectual capacity, leadership ability, and financial stability supplied his voids, and he masked manipulation in spiritual language. I questioned my own discernment. I was not being loved -- I was being conquered. But I didn't see it.

Not at first.

Then, the anesthesia wore off. Numbness was gone. Consciousness and all feelings returned to the surgical sites - my crushed, contrite spirit; my broken, hardening heart; and my disappointed, wounded soul. Salted with tears, my nightly pillow became my altar. "'Lord, You said in Your word the righteous cry to You and You deliver them out of all their troubles.' Lord, rescue ME!" I cried out for years. Then one night as tears saturated my pillow, the Lord said, "Daniel 10:12, Romans 4:3 and I John 1:9."

> *"Folice, From the moment you set your heart to understand and humbled yourself before me, your words were heard...Confess. I am faithful and just to forgive you and cleanse you from all unrighteousness. Abraham believed God and it was accounted to him as righteousness."*

Hope began to rise.

Then, He rescued me.

How did I get **here**?

I believed God. I took God at His Word. Oh, I would have fainted -- except **I believed** to see the greatness of the Lord in the land of the living.

# Bloom: Growth in the Unexpected Place

Journaling -- a lifeline, sacred ground, where I poured out the pain -- God met me-- in ink and intimacy. **Healing and hope happen here**, with trust-growing faith that God will lift my head, love my soul, and mend my heart.

I am **here** by grace. God, so wonder-full and merciful, used my broken vows, disappointed desires, and weary heart to teach me how much I am worth. I got **here** through the wilderness of warred abuse—emotional, spiritual, mental, and financial—but also through the apprehensive, yet wholehearted hope in God's Word; and through honest, truthful worship to my already all-knowing God. **Preparation happened here.**

I am **here** because of love. Unnumbed and fully feeling, I am humbly aware that I am *here* because God, whose love is never-ending, unconditional, and all-encompassing, used the flaws of my flesh and the conditions of my humanity, not to condemn, but to teach me that nothing—no relationship, falter, or trauma—can separate me, **or**

## Bloom: Growth in the Unexpected Place

**you**, from the love that Christ has for those who worship Him in spirit and in truth and for those who trust that no matter the cycles of pain, **purpose is prepared** through the challenges of the call, the empowerment of El Roi, and healing of the heart.

*R. Folice Bailey*

1. *Bloom when numbness fades and truth begins to rise.*
2. *Bloom when brokenness becomes the doorway to deliverance.*
3. *Bloom when God's love redefines your worth and restores your voice.*

# Bloom: Growth in the Unexpected Place

## R. Folice Bailey
## CEO Focus & Finish, LLC

*R. Folice Bailey is an experienced educator, certified professional coach, and business owner passionate about empowering beginning female principals and supporting special educators. With over a decade of coaching experience, she combines her leadership expertise with a heart for healing and spiritual growth. WholeHEARTed Devotional Journal was her first published work. As a creator of devotional journals and leadership manuals, Folice equips women and educational leaders with the tools to succeed, heal, and grow in purpose and intimacy with God. Her life and work are grounded in legacy, excellence, and faith.*

**www.focusfinish.com**
**www.rfoliceb.com**

# 6. Interlude: Hey Sis, Bloom!

Hey Sis...
The power of your tongue
has been silent too long.
But now,
you speak.

You speak with confidence,
with knowledge,
with ancestral wisdom.

A voice so strong,
it shakes the weak-hearted...
those too afraid of your mightiness
try to shrink you.

They condemn your words,
make you believe you're less than,
unworthy,
too much.

But Sis...
Speak loud.
Speak your truth.
Speak for the ancestors whispering through your

# Bloom: Growth in the Unexpected Place

belly.
Speak, Sis.
Speak.

Because through your words,
you birth generations
who are building healing legacies...
Rich minds,
rooted in emotional intelligence,
grounded in love.

Sis... you are enough.
Your voice is sacred.
Your heart is free.
Stop shrinking so others can feel tall.

Stop shaming your sister...
hold space for her to grow.
Because when one of us blossoms,
our communities shine brighter.
Our roots reach deeper.

The power of our words
waters the gardens
that the world tried to burn down.
When just one of us blossoms,
We feed the whole garden.
We plant more

and more
flowers.

Not just surviving...
but blooming.
In unity.
In wholeness.
In peace.

So, Sis... Speak.
Speak with dignity.
Speak with kindness.
Speak with love.
Because your voice,
is the seed
we've all been waiting for.

# Tamara "MsTeeKay" Kumoji

1. *Bloom, reclaim your voice as power, not apology.*

2. *Bloom when your authenticity nurtures community, not competition.*

3. *Bloom when your words become legacy.*

# Bloom: Growth in the Unexpected Place

## Ms. TeeKay
## Art Wellness Coach | Author | Poet
## International Speaker

With over 25 years in the arts, **Ms. TeeKay** blends poetry, storytelling, and stage presence to inspire and heal. A published author and keynote speaker, Ms. TeeKay's recent speech at the GSU International Speaker Experience in Athens, Greece, highlights her global impact. As co-founder of FYBR, LLC, she is dedicated to nurturing local talent and using words and creative energy to inspire and elevate others. Alongside her creative endeavors, she skillfully balances motherhood and entrepreneurship.

**www.Tamshandcrafts.com**

# 7. Give Yourself Grace to Grow and Go

*"When you finally learn that a person's behavior has more to do with their internal struggle than it ever did with you – you learn grace." - Allison Aars*

I accepted a leadership assignment on a team, unbeknownst to me, in a chaotic workplace. To the naked eye, there were few visible signs of rough waters ahead, yet beneath, an iceberg was gaining strength and momentum – dragging the culture like a ravenous lion clenching the dead carcass of its unwitting prey.

On the surface, the organization espoused values aligned with my core beliefs and demonstrated behavior both publicly and privately, which advanced our society. Yet, beneath lurked assumptions and fears that cultivated a culture prioritizing comfort over change and silence over substance.

# Bloom: Growth in the Unexpected Place

One afternoon, my manager delivered feedback that felt like a punch to the gut: "You need to take the initiative to bring thorny issues to the surface – at the appropriate time." Stunned, I realized this was a warning, and I barely held it together.

Later, I replayed every interaction, and amidst the chaos of my thoughts, a realization struck me: their behavior wasn't about me; it was a result of their internal struggle and reluctance to give and receive feedback. This was my chance to show grace—not just to them, but to myself.

At one of our virtual meetings, the small team gathered online, resembling the iconic squares of The Brady Bunch, each one marked by visible frustration. It was clear: we had reached a breaking point. I could feel my heart racing like a diver perched atop a 50-foot ledge; I steeled myself for the plunge beneath the surface, where my vulnerabilities would be revealed. I drew in a deep breath, undeterred; I poured out like an opened fire hydrant; "I am struggling," I confessed, my voice quivering with emotion. "I feel the weight of this work, and I need help to navigate."

One by one, my colleagues opened up. "I don't feel valued," one said. "My voice doesn't appear to matter." another confessed. The floodgates opened and we were no longer just colleagues; we were human beings grappling with our waves of doubt and uncertainty about the way forward. Subsequently, I learned a powerful lesson: vulnerability breeds connection. I realized that giving myself grace meant embracing my imperfections, not just for myself but for the team as well.

As leaders, we do more than plant seeds; we are expected to cultivate and nurture them, providing the essential care needed for growth. By creating environments where potential will blossom, ensuring each seed can flourish, ask yourself – what kind(s) of leader are you? Throughout my professional career, I have observed and exhibited qualities of transformational, democratic, and even transactional leadership—each with its impact.

Transformational leaders cultivate an environment of trust and share a compelling vision by addressing current issues and inspiring future generations to see beyond the present circumstances. Scholar and activist Angela Davis embodies these qualities. She has inspired generations to engage in social justice movements by reinforcing the idea that collective action can lead to substantial societal change.

Democratic leaders engage team members in decision-making, valuing diverse perspectives where these ideas can be nurtured and developed, leading to collective growth. On January 25, 1972, fellow Brooklynite and Sorority Shirley Chisholm delivered a powerful speech at my home church, Concord Baptist Church of Christ, launching her campaign for the presidency. With a distinct lisp and a radiant smile that showcased her imperfect teeth, she passionately proclaimed, "We Americans are a dynamic people, shaped by our rugged individuality and treasured diversity, driven by our belief in human dignity, and inspired by our generosity and goodwill toward one another." Chisholm's ability to inspire, despite the weight of societal issues, exemplifies how leaders can extend grace by recognizing and uplifting the potential within others.

Like Angela and Shirley – you, as a leader – are also a seed. What fruits are you bearing through your model of leadership? Just as you can identify a tree by its fruit, so you can identify people [leaders] by their actions. Effective leaders recognize their responsibility in nurturing the potential within their teams, creating an environment conducive to growth, and thriving. Consider how you might create a nutrient-rich environment to help others reach their full potential. Regardless of the specific needs, it is the gardener's [leader] responsibility to provide the right care and conditions necessary for each plant to bear good fruit.

This is your reminder to give yourself grace. As we support one another and engage in difficult conversations, we will till the right soil and thrive. Together, we can empower each other to grow and go.

# Dr. Shahara C. Jackson

1. ***Bloom when you break the silence.***
   *Choosing vulnerability in a toxic culture can transform colleagues into collaborators and turn isolation into authentic connection.*
2. ***Bloom when grace meets grit.***
   *Leadership is not just about pushing through; it's about embracing your own imperfections and extending grace—to yourself and others.*
3. ***Bloom when you lead like a gardener.***
   *Great leaders don't just plant seeds—they till the soil, remove the weeds, and create the conditions for others to grow, thrive, and bear fruit.*

# Bloom: Growth in the Unexpected Place

**Dr. Shahara C. Jackson**
**CEO, Chief Experience Officer, LyfPrints, Inc**.

*Leading with grace and love, **Dr. Shahara C. Jackson** believes that children and adults flourish in nurturing environments. Having graced stages on five continents, she uses her powerful speaking and singing voice to uplift and inspire. A proud graduate of Hampton University, CUNY - Baruch College, and Harvard University, Shahara's vibrant style creates unforgettable experiences. In 2012, she founded LyfPrints Inc., embodying the idea that every interaction leaves a life print—fingerprints represent the marks we leave on each other, while footprints symbolize the paths we create together. Dr. Jackson's work has impacted thousands, equipping them with renewed purpose and the tools to thrive.*

**www.linkedin.com/in/shaharacjackson**

# 8. I Choose Life, And I Speak Life

I've had intense and debilitating struggles with my faith. There were times when I had given up on God altogether. But regardless of my doubts, I had reminders of His love and care for me at every turn.

There was overwhelming evidence every day that, though I was flaky in my devotion to Him, He stayed consistent in His love for me. Although my faith journey has not been linear by any means, I am learning to trust God and honor Him in all that I do.

I practice doing this by trusting that there is no purpose, plan, or life that I can orchestrate for myself that is better or as good as the one that God has for me. I have confidence in knowing this truth is my solid foundation.

God sustains all of creation with His Word. That's how eternal and significant His Word is. His Spirit lives in me, the same Spirit that raised Jesus from the dead. That's how powerful and certain his authority over all things, including life and death, is.

His Spirit lives in me, and the power of life and death is in my tongue - so I choose life, and I speak life.

Whenever I speak a word over myself, acknowledge a truth after revelation from the Holy Spirit, or affirm and come into agreement with something that God has declared or stated about my identity, it seems like the forces of darkness do everything in their power to reverse it or "undo" what has been done.

But of course, such forces have no power over God's Spirit or my destiny, so they cling to my flesh and get me to self-sabotage.

I'm finally recognizing this pattern. I say, "I'm free," but by the end of the month, I feel more bound than ever before. I'd say, "I have peace and clarity," but then I am consumed by financial worry. I'd say,

# Bloom: Growth in the Unexpected Place

"I know who I am," then I start feeling insecure and doubt my ability to do anything; I start wondering if I'll ever be enough. I began to think that my words were less than meaningful or powerful; I began to think they were hollow, half-baked promises. I began to think to myself, "I should just stop talking so much. Even to myself."

I would think, stop making big declarations all the time because they don't mean anything. Thinking that my words and the confidence behind them were fruitless scared me because the last thing I wanted to become was someone whose words didn't mean anything at all.

I want my words to hold weight in the eyes of God and people.

I want to be dependable. I want to be trustworthy. While I should be selective about what I say and be intentional about the actions that follow my words, thinking that my words were anything less than powerful, life-changing tools that were potent in nature was a deceptive perception of my identity and authority in Christ. It's a downplaying of God's power and reveals a doubt in His Word—the same Word that gave birth to and sustains all creation.

This all clicked when I remembered what a girl said to me in a small group circle as we discussed our personal struggles in our faith journeys. I was talking about how I often felt inadequate, and the other girls in the circle were giving me advice on how *not* to allow the fear of inadequacy to consume me or be prioritized over my obedience to or trust in God. She said, "Don't let the enemy render you mute."

All God wants is a yes—and an obedient heart. Regardless of where I feel like my abilities or qualifications fall short of going to a higher place, his instructions and directions to go to that place qualify me. His creation-sustaining, dead-raising words are more than enough to qualify me for anything. Taking one step after another, trusting that God knows the path, even if I can't see beyond my limitations, carries me further than my own strength. It's okay if I can't see the fullness of the path that lies in front of me, only that I am willing and intentional about taking the next step.

# Zaria Blue-Hardy

1. *Bloom when you trust God's Word over your own doubt and speak life—even when darkness tries to silence you.*
2. *Bloom when you realize your voice holds power, not because of your perfection, but because His Spirit lives within you.*
3. *Bloom when you take the next step in faith, knowing God's yes qualifies you beyond your own strength or sight.*

# Bloom: Growth in the Unexpected Place

*Zaria Blue-Hardy is a twenty-year-old college student from Linden, NC. She is pursuing a bachelor's degree in English creative writing. She has also declared a minor in Biology to work towards a future career in dermatology. Her work weaves together storytelling and spiritual insight, drawing from faith-centered themes and the quiet strength found in healing, both of the body and the soul. As both a student of literature and science, she believes language holds the power to restore, redefine, and reconnect us to our true selves.*

*www.linkedin.com/in/zaria-blue-hardy*

# 9. Peaceful Tenacity

Professionally, I have considered the motto that all work has dignity. There is nothing more professionally rewarding than achieving self-reliance through honest work and support of one's family. My goal is to look at every achievement with gratitude and thanks. I've worked in education, project management, contract work, and temporary services, and have held positions including North Carolina notary, NC Works associate, administrative assistant, education assistant, and manager of furniture and retail stores. The goal was to continuously work to go forward to better my life.

There have been many challenges over the years. It is the Agape version of life –the highest form of love and forgiveness, which has supplied me the momentum to live along with the support of family and friends. During my years in the workforce, major events occurred, such as the fall of the Berlin Wall, the Twin Towers tragedy, hurricanes, and the pandemic of COVID-19. I've learned it is important to find peaceful tenacity, a belief, faith, and knowledge that there are more than the daily and weekly struggles of life. It is important to live, love, dance, and enjoy your life. Knowing yourself is important to get through the years and to appreciate the values you gain, the challenges are just that.

I have been privileged to know many people who were eclectic and brilliant. Many of them supported me through good times and struggles. It is important to respect these abilities to create a civilized and beautiful world. I respect formally educated and non-formally educated coworkers. I have learned as much from each and found that the ability to utilize knowledge is very important.

Overcoming struggles through truth and knowledge is one of the best goals to have in life. I have had a very good life, despite difficult moments, through the Power of Peaceful Tenacity. I do not look back on these moments as limitations or with belittlement. I was living as and able to make it better for others. Living with Peaceful Tenacity would be my masterpiece, so that others could overcome their difficulties.

The perfect world does not exist. Overcoming difficulties such as teenage years, divorce, bankruptcy, or major illnesses is difficult. Tenacity and audacity are the keys. It is the momentum of believing in God and family support that carries one through. I was lucky to have both.

What we overcome defines us as individuals as we live forward toward the future. I have decided to be mindful and enjoy the good days and happenings. When possible, I work with my community and church to build worthy causes and support efforts to make the world great. I continue to support nonprofit organizations now that I have retired. It is my desire to help through community service and small donations to charities.

I practice forgiveness each day and use the

knowledge I have gained to build the best life possible. It is important to provide positivism and growth for the future. As I build my business, I exercise Peaceful Tenacity, a belief, faith, and knowledge that there are more than the daily and weekly struggles of life.

# Kim Parks

1. *Bloom when embracing every role with dignity and gratitude.*
2. *Bloom through "Peaceful Tenacity"—faith, forgiveness, and mindful endurance.*
3. *Bloom by uplifting others—through community service, positivity, and continued growth.*

# Bloom: Growth in the Unexpected Place

**Ms. Kim D. Parks** is a professional writer and business owner based in Lexington, North Carolina. She has over 20 years of experience from the North Carolina University System and holds expertise in writing, transcription, and editing. Her industry knowledge spans clothing, retail, construction, project management, contracts, and marketing. Known for her adaptability and commitment to quality, Kim continues to evolve her skills to serve new and emerging industries.

**www.kd-consultant.com**

# 10. Every Day's a Good Day for a Positive Change

I have always been someone who roots for the seemingly underdog. I never really knew why until recently. There were so many things I was told I couldn't do growing up.

When I was about five years old, I was diagnosed with asthma. I spent a lot of time in the emergency room and on the fifth floor of one of the local hospitals. It seemed like everything triggered an attack—getting too hot or too cold, running, being around cigarette smoke, eating corn nuts, laughing too hard, and the list goes on.

This went on until around seventh grade. So, I don't have too many memories from childhood other than being in the hospital.

My faith has kept me.

I began asking the Lord to heal my emotions in my

# Bloom: Growth in the Unexpected Place

twenties. It has been a journey. More recently, I've been asking what I can learn from all I have experienced.

I've been planted in some interesting places.

Nine months ago, I started a deeper level of healing. The work is very necessary. The work is hard. Roots are being exposed, floodlights are finding lies I believed, and truth is being revealed.

I am growing in my ability to identify my emotions, express them, and have compassion for myself, my family, and my community.

There are many things I still don't know how to do.

Some of them might be considered basic; however, I was not taught them at a young age. I am now in my forties. As I have learned compassion for myself, I've also had to have a few conversations telling people I really don't know what's happening right now.

# Bloom: Growth in the Unexpected Place

Something I remember the Lord saying early on in this season, "your healing is connected to the destiny of some children who will be in your care." Some of the growth so far has been recognizing I have abandonment issues and not taking time to grieve the loss of each season.

I'm learning to slow down. In order to bloom, you must be planted and have water, sun, and a little fertilizer. Weeds (or lies) may also come up. Those need to be plucked up immediately.

I'm preparing to have children in my home. I'm making space for them. The spare bedroom was my office. I must downsize to make room. Some of the boxes in there have accompanied me on a few moves. There's no more room for them. I can't keep all this stuff.

Who knew purging and downsizing would be so emotional?

The items served their purpose for a season I'm no

longer in. It's okay to give them to someone else to use. I didn't know I would need to process the items as I took them out of each box and spoke about them verbally. I have more compassion for those who are downsizing—whether it be the elderly or those who hoard things.

In my journey, I have realized that in the United States, we often rush from one thing to the next and rarely take the time to sit and process our feelings. Some of the boxes that have been the hardest to open are related to teaching or missions. I started both in the early 2000s. I am still doing them, but they look very, very different now.

Change always means loss.

This is something with which I am just now connecting. These have been good changes, yet that means I had to stop doing something else — such as changing relationships, moving to a new location, changing schools, learning new systems, etc.

# Bloom: Growth in the Unexpected Place

I am still in missions, just on a home assignment. I am still teaching, just not confined to an elementary classroom, as the world is my classroom.

## Marteka Landrum

1. **Bloom when healing uncovers truth, not just pain.**
   *Because sometimes the truth is what sets you free—not the comfort, not the closure, but the clarity.*
2. **Bloom when letting go makes space for new purpose.**
   *Release isn't loss—it's preparation for alignment, growth, and divine redirection.*
3. **Bloom when compassion replaces perfection in your process.**
   *Because grace will take you further than grind ever could, and progress doesn't require punishment.*

# Bloom: Growth in the Unexpected Place

*Marteka Landrum* *is an academic life coach for teenagers. She works with schools and parents by meeting teens where they are to help them improve organizational skills and study habits, and to explore paths for after high school. Marteka received a Bachelor of Arts in Education from Wichita State University with certification in English as a Second Language. She is an Associate Certified Academic Life Coach with Coach Training EDU and is pursuing certification with the International Coach Federation. She loves to cook, sing, travel, and help others find their truth.*

**www.positivechanges11.com**

# 11. From Selling Flowers to Growing Communities

In my heart, I knew my mom never wanted me or a family. It hurts every day knowing that because when I needed a mother to talk to, there was no one to call. When she left my dad, I was four. She took us and moved in with her boyfriend. That boyfriend was abusive!

One day he took a belt and beat me across my entire body because I forgot to wash my hands after dinner. When I told my mom what happened, she said, "I probably deserved it" and went to bed with him. The pain and confusion to her reaction proved more painful than the actual beating. That was the first time my world was seriously crushed.

# Bloom: Growth in the Unexpected Place

At that point in my life, I had already seen and experienced a lot more pain and trauma than some people experience in a lifetime and a lot less than others experience in a minute. I used to think the details were important, but in the wrong mind, the details can be used as a weapon to repeat the trauma. I choose to focus on growth while acknowledging the darkness that created it.

I started my first business at age six. I picked the flowers at my apartment complex and went door-to-door selling them to the people who lived there. I priced them at 5 cents for a single flower and 10 cents for however many I had left in my hand. I picked them, I delivered them, and I brought joy to the people who purchased from me. Occasionally, I even managed to turn a rude person into a kind one. I created a product and a delivery service. This is how my journey from selling flowers to growing communities began.

There was a painted rock at one apartment that read "please turn me over" and six-year-old me

# Bloom: Growth in the Unexpected Place

happily obliged! To my delight, the other side said, "Ahhh. Thank you!" I thought the person who lived there must have been a lot of fun, so I tried to sell him some flowers. Well, he was quite rude to me and asked why he would pay for his own flowers since he lived in the apartments too, then told me never to knock on his door again. I was completely shocked, hurt, confused, and I felt guilty. I left crying.

I reminded myself how many people I was making happy with the flowers, and I avoided that apartment. One day I saw the "please turn me over" rock in the middle of the parking lot far away from the owner's apartment, so I took it back. I could have simply put it back at the front door and left, but six-year-old me thought an explanation was necessary. I knocked on the door, only to be yelled at again. I explained, apologized, gave the rock back, turned to leave, and started crying. Suddenly, his whole demeanor changed, and he realized I was trying to do the right thing. He purchased the whole bundle of flowers, apologized for being rude, and

# Bloom: Growth in the Unexpected Place

politely asked me not to come back again.

After selling flowers, I spent the next 10 years selling candy door-to-door, followed by a 20-year career in office administration and accounting while simultaneously maintaining multiple paid hobbies to balance and keep my sanity in life despite various instances of abuse.

Day by day, I made more genuine connections and met more people who supported me and what I was doing. I looked in that mirror and really got to know myself so that I could be as honest as possible with the people I serve, the people who support my goals, and the people who will benefit from me fulfilling my purpose. So much growth was accomplished just by giving myself time to reflect.

I have built a home and a community for myself and a physical location for The Funk! Creative Community Center where I am accepted, included, and appreciated. The Funk! is a space for artists, educators, and entrepreneurs who are educating, empowering, and growing creative communities. It has been less than a year since it opened, and the growth is so humbling. There are now over 25 unique individuals sharing this space to supplement their income, support their goals, and fulfill their purpose—plus hundreds of supporters around the world and growing daily!

I was able to provide a space for myself and others to grow in unexpected ways, improve their overall life balance, and share abundance. The Funk! in so many ways offers me the opportunity to share a small portion of the growth created!

*Joylyn*

1. *Bloom when past pain fuels purpose and compassion.*
2. *Bloom when reflection leads to personal and communal growth.*
3. *Bloom when you create space for others to thrive.*

*Originally known as **Joylyn**, I am an alleged human who is just doing my best to see myself clearly, reflect my true self, and fulfill my purpose. My life has been a series of experiences and journeys, with many more to come. I am from nowhere and everywhere, simultaneously in the spotlight and invisible. Currently, I own and operate The Funk! Creative Community Center and Belly Dance by Shaula in Lexington, NC.*

**www.BellyDancebyShaula.com**
**www.thefunkonline.com**

# 12. Soft Black Girl Life

Love after heartbreak was something I didn't think I'd be blessed to find—until, to my surprise, I met this fine chocolate brother who decided after six months that I would be his bride. I got a wonderful job right around the corner from my house. I was living my best life. But I often chose the harder way to do things because I didn't know any better.

I came from Southern Black women who sometimes made life more complicated than it needed to be. In my world, if it wasn't hard, it wasn't real. You had to be Superwoman to feel worthy of a pat on the back.

Everything around me, my upbringing, my sorority life, the household I grew up in—taught me that being aggressive was the only way to be effective. I was socialized to be a caregiver on every level.

The women who raised me carried a lot of trauma. That trauma made it hard for them to trust, and in turn, they developed entitlement issues. Those were the women who nurtured me—who helped me become just like them.

As the eldest daughter of seven, ordained clergy, a full-time employee, and an active member of Alpha Kappa Alpha Sorority, Inc.—joined during my time at Bennett College—my life was full. I also belonged to several sister circles and community organizations.

So, when the pandemic slowed everything down, I slowed down too. But what I didn't expect was to land on the sick and shut-in list. On December 21, 2021, I woke up unable to move my right hand and arm. At the hospital they said it was a muscle spasm, and I agreed—because I didn't recognize the severity of what was happening. I didn't even consider the possibility of a stroke.

Three days later, my husband, who's a health coach, took me back to the hospital and told them to check me for a stroke. I had survived one.

# Bloom: Growth in the Unexpected Place

At 23, I was diagnosed with a rare blood disorder called Antiphospholipid Antibody Syndrome. It's the reason I don't have living children. But that had always been invisible.

Shot number two of the COVID-19 vaccine took what had been private and made it visible. And just like that, I had to grieve my former normal. I was deeply attached to my freedom and independence.

My elders often glorified my youth because it symbolized time they'd lost. So, having control over my time became sacred to me. But with a visible disability—and strong spiritual gifts that made me discerning—I could feel everything shifting.

One day, a woman with her granddaughters looked at me strangely. I'm not elderly, but I walk with drop foot from the stroke, which affects my balance. That kind of attention is different. It's not the kind I was used to. That's when I had to release my idols. That cracked everything open.

# Bloom: Growth in the Unexpected Place

My mother—who is still living—gave me many things, one of them being an appreciation for aesthetics. She's an incredibly beautiful woman. So were her children. But because of mommy issues, I didn't always see myself in her. I didn't feel like her daughter. I didn't have the domestic skills—cooking, cleaning—that defined her. At best, I could do laundry.

Do you remember the movie *Soul Food*? Vivica could cook. Vanessa Williams? Not so much. That was me. I was the educated one, not the domestic one. It took therapy, spiritual direction, life coaching, sister circles, and the guidance of my pastor, Nicholas Johnson, to help me unravel that. Shoutout to Dottie's Butterflies, too.

Now, as a three-year stroke survivor, I've learned so much. Learning to love myself without placing value on what I used to—that was everything. Truly loving myself as I am, not how others thought I should be, opened the door to freedom.

# Bloom: Growth in the Unexpected Place

Like when I went to North Carolina for my cousin's watch party. Her husband asked, "Why didn't you stay here after college?" And I replied, "Because my siblings were small. I didn't want them not to know me." But after that trip, I realized how many of my life decisions had been based on obligation—not what was best for me. I wasn't even prioritizing myself in my own life.

It took a near-death experience to see how God made me—perfectly and wonderfully—even if I didn't look like the rest of my tribe. Now, six months away from turning 50, I'm living unapologetically. I'm living my Soft Black Girl Life.

*Isis Agyei*

1. *Bloom when survival teaches you to slow down, soften, and finally choose yourself.*
2. *Bloom when you release the pressure to perform and embrace healing instead.*
3. *Bloom when life rearranges your priorities— and reveals your worth was never in your grind, but in your grace.*

# Bloom: Growth in the Unexpected Place

*Reverend Isis Agyei* *is a natural-born servant leader and the youngest, first woman President of the East Orange Clergy Association. She was the first woman licensed at Christ Resurrection Missionary Baptist Church under the late Rev. Dr. Leora Liggins. A proud Bennett Belle, she joined Alpha Kappa Alpha Sorority, Inc. at Bennett College and is a life member. She is an alumna of RISE Together at Union Theological Seminary and Iron Sharpens Iron at Princeton Theological Seminary, where she earned a certificate in Executive Leadership. She is the beloved wife of Michael Kofi Agyei Jr.*

# 13. Interlude: When Love Beholds the Bloom

Most of the voices in *Bloom: Growth in the Unexpected Place* rise from the soil of womanhood—voices that have fought, healed, surrendered, and soared. But nestled within these pages is one voice that arrives gently from beside the garden, not within it.

It is the voice of a husband. A man who did not just walk alongside his wife's journey—he beheld her bloom. He witnessed the shifting and the mending, the silence, and the song. Through a season marked by medical struggle, he stood not as a savior, but as a sacred witness. With every setback she faced, he saw something sacred unfold, her blooming.

His voice is not an interruption, it's an illumination. His words are not present to explain her, but to honor her. They remind us that blooming is rarely a solitary act. Sometimes, it is cradled in quiet observation. Sometimes, it is seen beautifully and beheld through someone else's eyes.

By inviting him in, we expand the circle of growth. We acknowledge that love, in its truest form, does not demand the spotlight—it simply reflects the light it sees in another.

Let his offering be a tribute to every woman who ever bloomed under the gaze of someone who believed in her beauty and experienced her Bloom, her Growth in the Unexpected Place.

On the next few pages receive this husband's tribute to his wife.

*Dr. Timogi, Curator*

# 14. When She Bloomed, I Began to See

I used to think I knew what strength looked like. I believed it was about holding it all together—power through pain, endurance without pause, grinding until the goal was met. But then I watched my wife bloom, and everything I thought I understood about strength, love, and purpose began to shift.

When Isis and I first got married, she used to say, almost with a shrug, "I'm not a good cook." It was one of those small comments that can carry big stories—stories of self-doubt, comparison, and fear of failing in front of the people you love most. But one year, around the holidays, she decided to try something she had never done before: cook a whole turkey from scratch.

I remember watching her in the kitchen—nervous but determined. She researched every step, called her mom, and asked friends; she seasoned that bird

# Bloom: Growth in the Unexpected Place

like it was a sacred offering. That Thanksgiving, we sat at the table, and when I took the first bite, I knew I wasn't just tasting turkey. I was tasting transformation.

That meal wasn't just food—it was evidence. Evidence of her willingness to rewrite a narrative she had once believed about herself. And at that moment, I saw the quiet courage it takes to change the story you've told yourself for years. That's real strength.

There are so many ways Isis has bloomed over the years, some loud but mostly quiet. One bloom I never expected to impact me so deeply was her relationship with laundry. Yes, laundry. For the longest time, she resisted the idea of drop-off laundry service. She felt like she should be able to do it all. That asking for help—or outsourcing everyday tasks—was somehow a failure. But life kept happening. Her schedule got busier. Health challenges required more rest. And finally, one day, she said, "I'm going to drop the laundry off."

## Bloom: Growth in the Unexpected Place

It might sound small. But I knew what it cost her to let go of that expectation, to release the guilt and embrace grace. It was one of the most beautiful acts of self-respect I've witnessed. In choosing herself, even in something as ordinary as laundry, she reminded me that growth often means letting go—not just pushing forward.

Isis's health journey has been one of the greatest tests of strength I've seen. There have been days when her body was in pain, when energy was low, when the light at the end of the tunnel seemed far off. But she never gave up on herself. She didn't mask the struggle—but she didn't let it define her either.

Through it all, she has chosen to rise—not always quickly, not always visibly, but always fully. Her healing became her revolution. And for me, it became a revelation. Her blooming didn't just teach me about her. It taught me about love that doesn't need to be fixed—but to witness, about partnership that isn't about performance—but presence. About

# Bloom: Growth in the Unexpected Place

strength that doesn't always look like muscle—it often looks like softness, surrender, and small brave steps.

Because of Isis, I've become a different man. A man who pays attention to the quiet wins. A man who listens more than he speaks. A man who understands that support is not about rescuing—it's about standing beside someone while they rescue themselves.

Too often, men are taught to look for success, beauty, or productivity in women. But real power lies in how a woman picks herself up, rewrites her story, chooses her peace, and loves herself into wholeness. That's what I've seen in Isis. And that's what I now understand love to be.

To every woman who is blooming—publicly or in private—I see you. And to the men: it's not our job to shape her. It's our honor to support her. And if we're willing, to grow too.

## Bloom: Growth in the Unexpected Place

Watching Isis bloom didn't just reshape my view of her—it reshaped my purpose. I am here not to lead her path, but to walk beside her, water her roots, and celebrate every petal. And I wouldn't trade that for anything.

*Michael Agyei*

1. *Bloom when a man learns that love isn't control—it's bearing witness to her becoming.*
2. *Bloom when her quiet courage inspires his own growth, and he chooses presence over performance.*
3. *Bloom when he honors her unfolding, not by leading—but by watering her roots and walking beside her.*

*Isis and Michael Agyei*

# Bloom: Growth in the Unexpected Place

*Michael Agyei is a husband, transformational coach, and entrepreneur committed to helping individuals heal, grow, and walk boldly in their divine identity. With over a decade of experience in recovery, faith-based leadership, and development, Michael brings a culturally aware perspective to every space he enters. As the founder of Image Enterprises and co-creator of Image of God Wear, his work blends storytelling, faith, and fashion to empower others. He credits much of his personal evolution to the love and partnership of his wife, Isis Agyei, whose quiet strength, and courageous blooming continue to inspire his understanding of true love and leadership.*

**www.image-enterprises.com**

# 15. Lighten Up and Bloom

One of my favorite songs is by Erykah Badu, and it's called **"Bag Lady."** In it, she speaks to women carrying too much of life's weight and says, with wisdom wrapped in melody, "You gon' hurt your back, dragging all them bags like that." And like many women who heard the tune I knew, she was talking to me, too.

I used to carry bags - heavy ones. Baggage packed with feelings of abandonment, rejection, resentment, and grief. You couldn't always see them on my shoulders, but they weighed me down just the same. My back wasn't bent over like the woman in the bible, but my spirit was.

I carried the weight of a father who abandoned me as a teen until his death. That kind of absence lingers. It creeps into your psyche, it echoes in your silence, and it convinces you that you have to prove

# Bloom: Growth in the Unexpected Place

you're worth loving. So, I performed, I overachieved, I worked for proof of my worth. I smiled through storms and let very little shake me. But that baggage...It was there.

Then came the marriage that looked good on paper, but in private, it consumed me. I married someone who couldn't love me deeply, couldn't see me fully, and over time, attempted to shrink me. That marriage ended in divorce, and while divorce brought relief, it also came with its own baggage: failure, regret, and fear. It launched me into single motherhood without a job.

Then there was work. The kind of workplace that doesn't value your output and ignores your passion. I gave it my ideas, my creativity, my time—but it only gave me a minimal paycheck and became a routine not a calling. I watched a system reward mediocrity. And still, I carried those feelings too. One day, I realized something: I was missing my bus.

I was missing my breakthroughs. I was missing my

passion. I was missing simple daily opportunities for joy and essentially, my destiny. Not because I wasn't capable—but because I had "too much stuff." Erykah said it best: *"You can't hurry up... you got too much stuff."*

And then, Scripture reminded me of two important directives. First, 1 Peter 5:7 *"Cast your cares, your anxieties, your pressure, on to God because He cares for you."* To cast means to throw it back, take one last look at it, toss it, and release your weight into an unknown abyss too large, too vast for you to have any control over it. So, cast.

Next, I was reminded in Luke 9:3, where Jesus sends the disciples out and says, *"Take nothing for the journey—no staff, no bag, no bread, no money, no extra shirt."* Just go. So that's exactly what I did. I started my journey with bare minimum tangible essentials but abundant faith, hope, and love.

Some things require a light load. Some destinations can't be reached when you're burdened, weighed down, and cumbersome. Some assignments require you to walk free—uncluttered, unhindered, and unburdened.

Unforgiveness, bitterness, and hate must be released, or you will heal the surface over an infected wound essentially sealing in pain and poison. Growth is not just about healing, it's about releasing. The releasing is the catalyst to the healing.

It was about letting go of the story I kept telling myself about who left, who didn't love me right, who didn't see my value. Letting go of the need to be perfect, tough, or "fine" you know, being the strong friend. Letting go of the past—not because it didn't happen, but because it already did and there is absolutely nothing, I can do about it! So, I started unpacking. I lightened my load.

I unpacked the grief that came with having a father who discarded me like I was nothing. I meditated on the scripture that when your mother and father

# Bloom: Growth in the Unexpected Place

forsake you God will take you up, and He did. I gave myself the permission to grieve and grow.

I unpacked the emotional bruises from a loveless marriage. I stood in the mirror, with no makeup and no mask, and told myself the truth: You are worthy. Still. Anyway. Always. Period.

I unpacked the frustration from giving years to a job that didn't see me, and I gave myself back to myself. I reclaimed my voice, my creativity, and my peace. I began building my life, my business, and my happiness. And when I let go of the bags, do you know what happened? I bloomed.

Not overnight. Not instantly. But beautifully. I am walking in the Grace of God.

I bloomed in my voice, in my purpose, in my presence. I stood taller—not because the ground changed, but because I wasn't hunched over by what I used to carry.

So, hear me clearly: Don't miss your bus. Don't miss

# Bloom: Growth in the Unexpected Place

your next because you're still dragging your yesterday's as dead weight. Don't miss your peace because you're still clutching the pain of the past. Don't miss your purpose because your hands are too full of what already happened. It's over.

Pack light. Pack with your purpose in mind.

Let go of what no longer serves you. Release the weight of anything that makes you question your worth. Drop the bags that aren't even yours to carry. Because healing isn't just about feeling better, it's about traveling lighter.

And when you do, you'll bloom. You'll step lighter. Navigate life more confidently. You'll speak with authority. Because you won't just be healed... you'll be free.

And that freedom—that's where love lives. That's when your life begins to radiate joy, confidence, and purpose.

So go ahead, Sis. Unpack. Release. Bloom.

# Bloom: Growth in the Unexpected Place

## Dr. Timogi

1. *Bloom when you unpack the pain, not just relive it.* Because healing isn't just remembering what hurt—you have to release it to reclaim your power.
2. *Bloom when you realize your past is not your purpose.* You're not here to carry what happened—you're here to grow from it, speak through it, and bloom beyond it.
3. *Bloom when you finally put the bags down.*
   Freedom begins where baggage ends—lighten your load, and your purpose will rise.

### *CEO, Create & Facilitate*

*Dr. Timogi is an Empowerment Strategist with two decades of corporate leadership and higher education experience combined. She is the author of 15 books and facilitates Customized Training Solutions for government, nonprofit, higher ed, and corporate agencies. As a keynote speaker she has graced stages from prisons to Harvard. She is an experienced faculty and student affairs member in higher education, District Manager in Corporate America, and Executive Director in the non-profit sector.*

*www.DrTimogi.com*
*www.CreateAndFacilitate.com*

# Bloom: Growth in the Unexpected Place

## About the Curator

## "I lead individuals and organizations from Elusive to Empowered."

Dr. Timogi is a Master Facilitator and Executive Coach and International Speaker with experience in corporate, nonprofit, and higher education leadership. She is the founder of Create & Facilitate, a North Carolina HUB Certified Customized Training Solutions Agency, specializing in personal and professional development, workshops, leadership retreat facilitation, and employee mediation. As an international keynote speaker, Dr. Timogi has inspired and trained diverse audiences, ranging from correctional facilities to prestigious institutions like Harvard. She is also the author of 15 books and numerous customized training programs, demonstrating her commitment to empowering individuals and organizations worldwide.

**Bloom: Growth in the Unexpected Place**

# Book Dr. Timogi Today!

Leadership Training and Development

Keynote Speeches

Panel Discussions and Panel Moderator

Executive Coaching

Individual and Group Coaching

Conferences

Employee Training and Development

Commencements

Workplace Conflict Mediation

Retreats

Customized Certifications

## CONTACT INFORMATION
PO Box 334
Lexington, NC 27293
www.DrTimogi.com
www.CreateAndFacilitate.com